CORY STORIES

A Kid's Book About Living with ADHD

by Jeanne Kraus
illustrated by Whitney Martin

MAGINATION PRESS • WASHINGTON, DC

To Cory, with love — JK

For my sons, Roddy and Whitney, with love always — WM

Published by
MAGINATION PRESS
An Educational Publishing Foundation Book
American Psychological Association
750 First Street, NE
Washington, DC 20002

For more information about our books, including a complete catalog, please write to us, call 1-800-374-2721, or visit our website at www.maginationpress.com.

The text type is Comic Sans.
Printed by Worzalla, Stevens Point, Wisconsin.

Library of Congress Cataloging-in-Publication Data

Kraus, Jeanne.
Cory stories : a kid's book about living with ADHD /
written by Jeanne Kraus ; illustrated by Whitney Martin.
p. cm.
ISBN 1-59147-148-6 (hardcover : alk. paper) — ISBN 1-59147-154-0 (pbk. : alk. paper)
1. Attention-deficit hyperactivity disorder—Juvenile literature.
I. Martin, Whitney, 1968- . II. Title.
RJ506.H9K73 2004
618.92'8589—dc22   2003028199

Manufactured in the United States of America
10 9 8 7 6 5 4 3

Hi! My name is Cory, and this is my story.
All of my life I've felt like a different kind of guy.
Mom and Dad say I'm just me, my very own Cory self.
Whatever that means!

Did you ever feel like there's a jumping bean inside of you even when you are trying to sleep? I do!

I feel wiggly and itchy almost all the time!

I love to be excited, but sometimes I get too excited. I wish I had a power switch, like the TV. Then I could turn myself off. (CLICK!)

Kids make fun of me sometimes, and I can't always figure out why.

Sometimes I cry when
my feelings get hurt.
All kids do that.
But it seems like
other guys don't get
their feelings hurt
as much as I do.

I'm not exactly
a tough guy,
even though
I try to act like one.

I have trouble making friends. I want to be a good friend, but lots of times I feel so jumpy inside that I can't calm down.

I have one favorite friend, and he's wiggly a lot too, just like me. Mom says I have radar for kids like me!

I have tons of great ideas, but it's hard to explain all of them. That is pretty frustrating!

Sometimes I talk before I think, and then I say something that gets me in trouble. I'm not trying to annoy people. But there are so many words and thoughts crowded into my head. They just keep pouring out.

Some guys are really good at sports. I'm a little bit good at soccer. It's so hard to pay attention for the whole game.

At recess, I'm always worried that I'll get picked last for teams. It seems like I have so many things to worry about!

Dad says I have a short attention span. That means it's hard for me to keep thinking about just one thing for a long time like other kids do.

Here's what happens at school: I don't pay attention to things I am supposed to (like my teacher giving directions), but I do pay attention to things I am not supposed to (like the paper clip in my desk that can be bent into a really cool airplane).

TODAY I AM GOING TO REMEMBER EVERYTHING!

Some days, I forget to do my chores and my homework, and my parents get mad. It makes me mad, too.

I try not to forget. I wake up every day and say, "Today I am going to remember everything!"

GONE

But then something happens and I can't. My remembering gets pushed out of my brain.

Being me can be hard work!

My bedroom and my backpack keep getting messed up.
My parents help me organize my stuff once a week so that
I know where everything is. Well, almost everything...

Yesterday my belt, my pencil, and my shoe just disappeared.
(Mom helped me find them. They were under my bed.
I also found a jacket I've been looking for.)

Stuff happens when I'm around. At dinner, milk spills, all by itself. My fork and spoon fall on the floor more than everyone else's.

Sometimes my whole body
falls off the chair.
I don't know how that happens!

At school my pencils and
papers skydive off my desk.
Go figure that out!

Writing neatly is impossible.
My pencil doesn't work right.

And scissors, they never cut
in straight lines.

Kindergarten wasn't too bad,
but in first grade
everything made
me MAD.

I was frustrated and sad a lot.
It was pretty embarrassing.

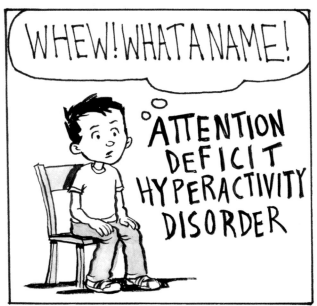

Mom and Dad wanted to help me, so they took me to a special doctor. She told me I have something called ADHD. That stands for Attention Deficit Hyperactivity Disorder. Whew! What a name!

The doctor said that the problems I was having were not my fault. She said that when kids have ADHD their brains just work a little differently from most other kids'. She said it's like having a car with a gas pedal stuck on "go."

That's why my motor is always running and my body moves before I know what it's doing and words come out of my mouth before I think about them.

WHAT A RELIEF!
Now I know why I feel like I do.

The doctor even said there are probably other kids at my school who have ADHD too, maybe even in my class. That means I'm not so different from everyone else!

The doctor gave me some medicine. She told me and my parents that the medicine would help me pay attention better. Also, it would help me feel not so wiggly on the inside. I was pretty excited about that. So were my mom and dad.

But that's not all. She also told my parents that I needed to go see another kind of doctor, too, a talking doctor. The talking doctor would help me learn how to feel better about myself and how to make some better choices.

My talking doctor had lots of great ideas.

I found out there are a lot of things I can do to help myself. There are some things my parents can do to help me at home, and even my teacher can help. That can make school lots more fun for me!

Mom helps me organize my backpack and my study area.

Dad helps me start my homework each day and lets me use a timer to make sure I am working when I am supposed to.

He also taught me
to take work breaks so
I could concentrate longer.

Both of my parents put notes up all over the house to remind me of my chores I need to do. I check off my jobs after I do them.

That feels good!

Our family has been through millions of sticker charts. I can earn points for doing all my chores. It took me a long time to get the hang of it. But now, sometimes I do my work without anyone telling me!

I found out that I get too close to kids' faces sometimes, and they don't like that.

My talking doctor told me to pretend that there is an invisible square drawn around other kids to remind me to step back when I am talking to them. It's called their body space. It worked!

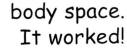

I also learned that when I see kids laughing, it doesn't mean they are laughing at me.

If I get upset, I have so many people I can talk to.

My talking doctor gives me
good ideas to help me
with my feelings.

My parents and I practice
what to do the next time
I have a problem. We practice
and practice!

My teacher
and I set
daily goals
for me.
At the end
of the day
we talk
about the
progress
I made.

And I found out that not everyone is always good at sports. Guess what? We found out I was good at other stuff.

I joined a kids' bowling club, and we bowl like crazy. I made some new friends, too.

I am good at concentrating in my karate class. I do an awesome roundhouse kick.

I'm pretty sure I will be a
great musician some day.
My piano teacher says
I am very talented.
I can play in two speeds,
fast and very fast!

At school and at home,
I can use the computer
for my work.
I am a whiz on the computer.
I am such an expert
that I even help Dad.

Mom and Dad came to school for a conference with Mrs. Smith. Know what?

Mrs. Smith says I am doing better in school.

She says I listen more to directions.

I improved at finishing my work.

My papers are a lot neater.

My parents were really proud. So was I!

You know what else?
I have some new friends.
Not just school friends
but karate friends and
neighborhood friends too.

Mom and Dad told me that there are so many good things about me. They said that...

I am a loyal friend. Everyone knows they can count on me.

I'm very good at math. I even help other kids with their work.

I have a great sense of humor. I can make people laugh.

I'm a teddy bear kind of a guy. That means I really like hugs, and Mom says that's a very good thing.

Dad says I'm sensitive. "Sensitive" means I care about other people and how they feel.

I care about animals, too. My cat Misty likes it when I relax my body. She lies on my stomach then, because she likes kids when they are calm.

Sometimes petting Misty real slow helps me quiet down. We kind of help each other.

Now I know that nobody needs to be good at everything.

But I found out that I am good at a lot of things.

And that's a great thing to know.

LIFE IS LOOKING GOOD!

NOTE TO PARENTS

by Jane Annunziata, Psy.D.

Cory's "stories" highlight a number of challenges that children may face when they have attention deficit hyperactivity disorder, as well as solutions that make living with ADHD easier. This book is intended to show children that they are not alone in these challenges. More than that, such challenges can be met head-on with help from others and with a broad range of skills that your child can learn, especially with love and support from you.

Like Cory, children with ADHD often cope with any of the following:

- high energy level, restlessness
- impulsive behavior
- speaking before thinking
- emotional sensitivity
- lack of awareness of social cues
- short attention span
- disorganization
- forgetfulness
- distractibility
- lack of physical coordination
- inability to complete projects

Treatment for these symptoms involves developing social and organization skills with the help of parents and teachers, and often includes psychotherapy or counseling, and medication. Without help, children can suffer socially and academically, which leads to poor self-image and increased risk for emotional and behavior problems.

It's important for kids to remember that they are as smart as any other kids, and that they can be gifted with artistic creativity, a great sense of humor, loyalty to friends and family, and compassion for others. Focus on the positives, and steer children toward activities where they are most apt to be successful and feel better about themselves.

As parents know, structure, rules, and schedules are vital for staying organized, finding and remembering things, getting things done on time (or at all!), and maintaining discipline. These roadmaps through the day help keep everyone on track. Parents can also help by setting realistic goals and developing habits with their children. Offer friendly reminders using lists, bulletin boards, and sticky notes. Have predictable times and places for things. Encourage success, and be specific with praise.

Use sticker charts as part of your goal-setting strategy, and offer positive reinforcement at the end of each day. Daily rewards should not be excessive: a cool pencil or sticker, a small toy. A trip to the dollar store after earning a certain number of stickers can be a good motivator. Rewards can also be experiences, such as picking dinner the next night from a few options or doing something new together. A few cautions: Don't turn experiences that should be "givens" into rewards, and keep in mind that such things as letting the child stay up later at night can backfire. Finally, earned rewards should *never* be taken away as punishment.

Anticipate problems before they arise. If your child is going to attend a birthday party, for example, invite him to sit down with you and talk about any problems that might come up. Help him think about what to expect and act out solutions with him. Afterward, discuss how things went, and focus on what went well. Encourage him to be persistent and not give up; you'll be there to offer support, as well as concrete guidance and suggestions.

Therapists and counselors can also be of tremendous help for kids, helping them talk through problems and work on skills. They can also help parents work optimally with their children. Other professionals, such as tutors, can assist with specific areas of the child's life. And finally, networks and support groups for both children and parents are great resources.

All children do best when their parents build positive, loving relationships with them, and this is especially so for children with ADHD. Because their lives usually involve a lot of correcting and problem solving, it's important that families also build plenty of fun activities and rituals into their day. Examples include regular one-on-one outings with each parent, dining together as a family as much as possible, baking brownies or washing the car or walking the dog together, Friday night pizza and a family video, and so on.

And always, a sense of humor is one of the most valuable tools a parent can have.

Here are some additional tips for specific problem areas:

Social Skills

For all children, having friends to play with is important. But sometimes kids with ADHD can have problems making and keeping friends due to impulsiveness, sensitivity, poor anger management, and other behavior problems. High sensitivity can lead to hurt feelings and can also make a child an easy target for bullies. And situations involving team sports can be extra hard because the pressures are stronger than in other social situations. Children with ADHD may not be able to focus closely on the game or be as well coordinated as their peers, and may suffer from teasing or be treated badly by people who are more interested in winning than in being good sports. Here are a few ways to help:

- Try to arrange get-togethers with just one friend at a time. One-on-one works best.
- Having a new friend over to your house at first is often more successful than going to the friend's house. Gradually work toward going to the friend's house by starting with short play dates there.
- Help your child see his role in a problem, with the focus being that he is not power-less and can help effect a better outcome next time.
- Get teachers and coaches involved to what extent they can in supporting your child's social skills and friendships. Teachers usually know about an ADHD diagnosis, but remember to share this information with coaches, camp counselors, and so on.
- Discuss and role play ways to respond to teasing and bullying so as to avoid hurt feelings and impulsive, angry behavior that can get your child in trouble.

- Arrange for your child to help with charitable organizations, such as soup kitchens, food drives, and toy drives. This is empowering for all of us; kids with ADHD especially benefit.
- Join clubs and organizational activities such as scouting, where the focus is not on winning.
- Choose sports that are more individually competitive, such as swimming and track.
- Try martial arts; these activities can help build skills of discipline and attention and well as coordination
- Find activities in which your child can excel, such as drama, music, or art if he is creative, or those that capitalize on his specific abilities and interests.

School Adjustments

Children with ADHD are usually average or above average in intelligence. However, academic and behavioral problems can affect their performance.

- Have your child keep a daily planner, initialed by the teacher.
- Teach your child how to empty his backpack every morning when he gets to school so that there is no rummaging.
- Keep a heavy plastic organizational folder for parent notes and homework in the backpack.
- At home, keep the homework area free from distraction, and make sure that all supplies are there.
- Help your child break homework into manageable chunks, starting with the least favorite subject.
- Communicate with the teacher if homework takes too long each night.
- Praise your child for starting independently, staying on task, and putting things away when finished.
- Set goals together with the teacher, such as, "raise your hand before you speak." These goals can be reinforced with a sticker chart.
- Have a plan of action for times that are less structured, when trouble is most likely to happen—recess, lunch, waiting for the bus, periods between classes, and special classes such as PE and art. Again, success at these times can be reinforced, but tackle one trouble area at a time.

Teachers should not punish by withholding recess. Children with ADHD need to be able to move around during the day, and taking away recess will result in restless energy in the classroom later in the day, as well as anger over the loss, which can lead to more misbehavior.

Attention Span

Kids with ADHD can have a hard time with both verbal and written directions, and with sticking with tasks that aren't very interesting to them. On the other hand, they may "hyperfocus" and get lost for hours in activities such as television and video games. Here are a few ways to keep them on track:

- Limit time with TV, computer, and videos, and enforce the limits.
- Physical exercise is always beneficial!

- Take short, timed breaks from tasks such as homework and chores.
- Encourage reading, board games, family talks and activities, and educational programs that you watch and discuss together as a family.
- Model good listening. Put everything aside and give full attention to your child, making eye contact and asking him for the same in return.
- Always praise your child when he gives you undivided attention.

Jane Annunziata, Psy.D., is a clinical psychologist with a private practice specializing in children and families in McLean, Virginia. She is also the author of several books for children on such topics as ADHD, adoption, and play therapy.

ABOUT THE AUTHOR

JEANNE KRAUS is an educational specialist with expertise in ADHD. She has served on educational task forces and developed presentations on ADHD awareness. A frequent speaker at conferences and workshops, she presents on such topics as organizational and study skills, parenting, and classroom management tips and instructional strategies for teachers. Ms Kraus has been an elementary school teacher in Broward County, Florida, for over 20 years. She is the mother of two sons, one of whom inspired this book.

ABOUT THE ILLUSTRATOR

WHITNEY MARTIN's illustrations appear in books, magazines, and catalogs, and he has worked on many animated film projects, including several Walt Disney movies. Before his career as an artist, he was a Sergeant in the U.S. Marine Corp Reserves. He now lives in Santa Fe, New Mexico, with his wife and two children.